A SPECIAL GIFT FOR

....

FROM

....

D1126516

For Mickey, the love of my life.
For Gabrielle and Isaac, the apples of my eye.
For Julie and Angie, our children's birth mothers
with whom we share a bond forever.
This is our orchard.

Text and illustrations © 2014 by Colleen D.C. Marquez

Published in the United States by Cupola Press®

www.cupolapress.com

Library of Congress Control Number: 2013940931

ISBN-13: 978-0-9857932-4-1

First Edition   10 9 8 7 6 5 4 3 2 1

Printed in Malaysia

A Gift for Little Tree

Colleen D.C. Marquez

Illustrations by

Masako Dunn

Cupola PRESS®

Lafayette, California

nce upon a springtime, an apple orchard buzzed with life. White flowers burst from every branch of every tree. Bees and hummingbirds danced from blossom to blossom. The air was sweet with the promise of apples for all.

The farmer loved his orchard. He walked among the trees, smiling as he examined the flowering branches. The trees knew his touch, and the leaves quivered with joy.

Each day, the farmer woke before sunrise to water his trees. Each week, he cleared weeds from around their trunks. In winter, the farmer sheltered the orchard from the frost. And year after year, he pruned the trees so they would be healthy and strong.

In the summer, the lacy blossoms gave way to tiny buds, and the orchard swelled with apples of many colors.

There were green apples and golden
apples, yellow apples and red apples.
Every tree had a special purpose.

There were trees with sweet apples for salads.
There were trees with tart apples for pies.

Other trees had soft apples for applesauce and apple butter. Still others grew crisp apples, which were delicious with cheese for the farmer's lunch.

In the autumn, as the farmer prepared for harvest, the trees stood tall, holding out their branches for him to see. The farmer nodded.

All the trees were happy; that is, all but one.

The little tree in the center of the orchard tried not to care as she watched the other trees hold their apples high. She had no apples of her own. Oh, how she longed to grow apples! Her longing grew stronger and stronger until Little Tree hurt inside from her top branch down to her roots.

The Grannysmith apple tree whispered: "She shouldn't try so hard! She should relax and just let it happen." The snappy red Fuji tree remarked: "Maybe you aren't supposed to make apples." But even if they meant well, their comments hurt Little Tree. Whenever she heard such things, her branches would droop, and her whole trunk would ache.

One day, when the farmer lingered longer than usual in the orchard, Little Tree rustled her leaves to catch his attention. "Farmer," she asked, "Why am I here if I can't grow apples? What am I to do?"

The farmer reached out to touch her smallest branch. "I am the one who planted you, Little Tree," he said. "I have not forgotten you." With this, Little Tree lifted her branches a bit higher.

When it was time to prune, the farmer trimmed away old wood and spindly twigs. He shaped the branches to make them strong. When he came to the green Pippin, his prized apple pie tree, he saw that the weight of her branches was too much for her to bear. "What will happen to me, Farmer?" the green Pippin asked. "With next year's apples, my branches will be so heavy, I'm afraid they will break!"

I have a plan," the farmer assured her. "I can lighten your load by grafting a part of you onto Little Tree. The two of you can form a special bond and grow beautiful apples together." The green Pippin marveled at the farmer's plan. "Thank you," she said.

Green Pippin bravely held out her branch. The farmer gently removed a growing bud, then pruned her back to health.

The farmer returned to Little Tree. "See," he said, "I have not forgotten you. Here is a gift from the green Pippin tree. Her branches were too heavy, and she cannot carry as many apples next season. With her gift, I have a way for you to grow her apples on your own branches."

Little Tree remembered her dream to have apples of her own unique color and flavor. The farmer's plan was different from her own. Could she possibly love apples that came from another tree? But she trusted the farmer. "Oh, Farmer, you know my heart! Thank you!"

The farmer took his knife and carefully carved an opening onto one of Little Tree's branches. He placed Green Pippin's bud into the fresh cut, wrapped it tightly, and instructed Little Tree: "Embrace this bud, and let your hope be strong. Together we will wait for spring."

Little Tree held onto the new bud with all her strength. With her leaves she sheltered it from the rain. When the wind blew, she rocked it softly. After what seemed like an eternity, the bud opened, and a small shoot of green peeked through.

With showers and sunshine, spring blossoms once again burst in the orchard. Little Tree delighted in the fragrance around her. She welcomed the dance of the bees and hummingbirds like never before.

On the first day of summer, Little Tree woke to see the farmer smiling as he admired her new branches. To her surprise, she saw tiny green apples forming where the lacy blossoms had been. "Are those my apples?" she asked. The farmer smiled.

This was the moment Little Tree had waited
for all her life! It did not matter that the
fruited branch came from another tree.
From the moment the farmer grafted the
bud to her limb, she loved it as her own.
The farmer's plan was better than she imagined.
How grateful she was to the farmer and to
the great green Pippin. How she swayed her
branches whenever the farmer walked by!

The seasons changed. It was once again time for pruning. This time, the farmer's sweet Honeycrisp tree bowed too low with fruit, so the farmer took a bud from her heavy branches and brought it to Little Tree. The next year, Little Tree bore both green Pippin and red Honeycrisp apples. It was a miracle!

For many years, the farmer grafted new buds onto Little Tree's branches. True to his word, the bond between the apple trees grew and grew. Little Tree, who had once been bare, became one of the most colorful trees in the orchard.

In the gentle breeze, Little Tree rocked her apples
and told them the stories of how they came to her.
Green Pippin and Golden Delicious, tangy red Fuji and
sweet Honeycrisp, apples of mixed colors and apples
of every flavor, Little Tree loved each one.

Behold, I have carved you on the palms of my hands.

ISAIAH 49:16

AUTHOR'S NOTE

I never considered adopting, not even after four
long years of infertility. Until I met Little Tree.

She was growing in a nursery, a bare root apple
tree with grafted branches, designed by her grower
to produce three different kinds of apples—all on
one tree! The nursery called her a 3-n-1 apple tree, but for me, she
was an "Adoption Tree". This was the *perfect* celebration gift for our
friends who had just adopted their first child.

Later that evening, I awoke with a middle-of-the-night inspiration
to write a story about this little tree. As I labored over the words,
I felt my heart stretch in surprising ways.

Before I wrote *A Gift for Little Tree*, I didn't understand how I could
love a child who wasn't from our own family tree. But by the early
morning, when my husband found me surrounded by drafts of story
and paper, my heart began to see.

Within that same year, my husband and I began building our own
family through adoption. Truly, from the moment our children were
grafted into our lives, placed into our arms by their gracious birth
families, we loved them as our own.

With great gratitude and love, and hope in the Farmer's faithfulness
for you, I am excited to share Little Tree's story.

Colleen D.C. Marquez
www.giftforlittletree.com

SPECIAL THANKS TO

···

Nightlight® Christian Adoptions
Serving families for over 50 years with domestic, international
and Snowflakes® Embryo Adoption services.
www.Nightlight.org | www.Snowflakes.org